My name is Sofia. **I'm new at my school.**
I've made some good friends and my teacher is cool.

School should be wicked and awesome, but sadly along came **a bully named Imogen Baddley.**

I never complain much –
I try to be nice,
but Imogen told all my friends
I have lice.

The day before that
she dropped ice down my neck...
My nerves were on edge –
I was really a wreck.

Wherever I stood, she was **right in my face.**
I wished she would vanish to some other place.

Her tricks were upsetting –
she didn't play fair,

like the **FROGS**
in my locker

and **JAM** on my chair.

None of the teachers
paid any **attention.**
She never was punished
or given detention.

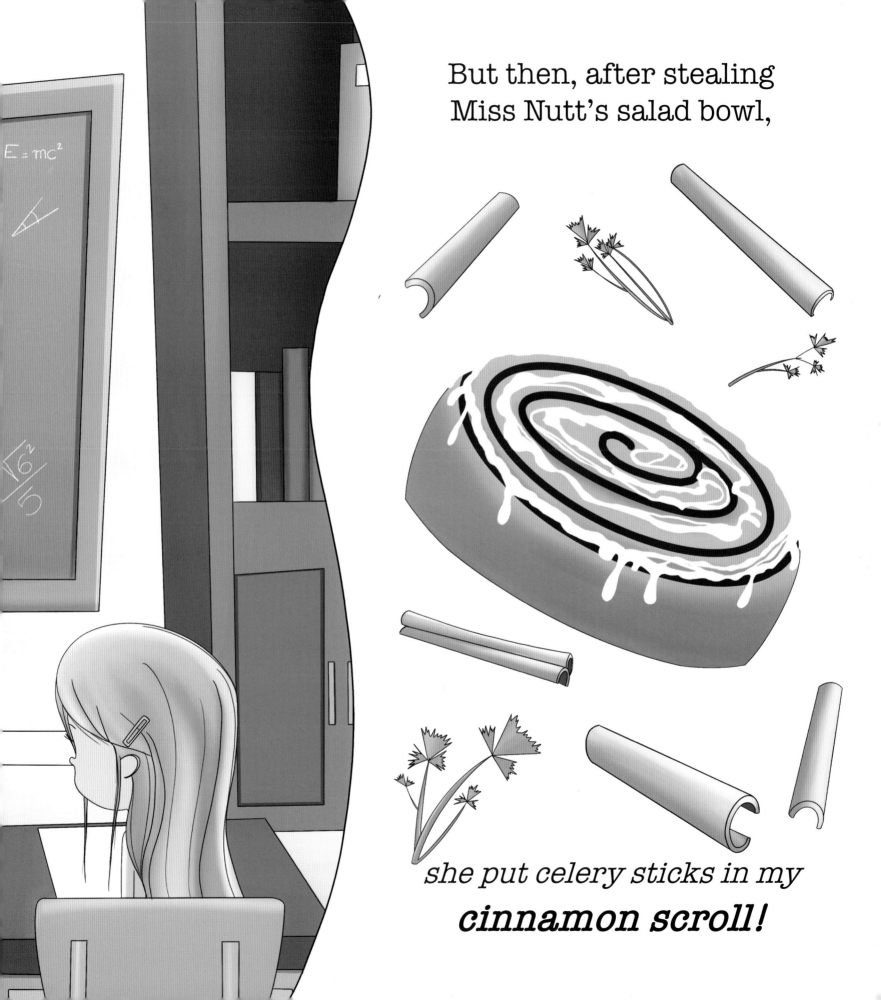

But then, after stealing Miss Nutt's salad bowl,

she put celery sticks in my ***cinnamon scroll!***

Of all the gross tricks **causing horror and fear,**
like sticking wet bubblegum into my ear,

the moment I finally lost all control

was when Imogen
messed with my
**cinnamon
scroll.**

As soon as I bit on a celery stick
I gasped and I shuddered – **I almost got sick.**

The very next day after two or three classes,
Imogen Baddley ran off with my glasses.

She sneakily buried them

under the sand...

...so I walked up to her and grabbed hold of her hand.

"Thank you!" I cried, **"That was very well done!**
The hunt for my glasses was serious fun."

Imogen glared and looked **highly annoyed**,
but seeing her cross was a look I enjoyed.

Later, she stole my banana at lunch...
"Tomorrow..." I promised, "I'll bring **the whole bunch!**

Perhaps you are hungry... **Do you want a hug?"**
She mumbled "No way", and walked off with a shrug.

The following day she arrived with a box.
She wanted to scare me **right out of my socks.**

She placed her **pet python**
on top of my lap

But I said, ***"He's so cute!"***
with a smile and a clap.

On Thursday she covered my hair
with thick honey.
I started to laugh –
like I thought it was funny.

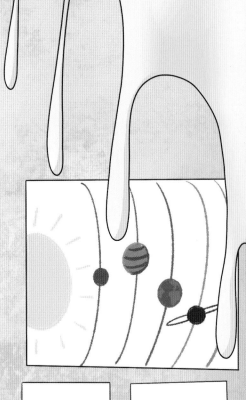

I tasted the honey
by licking my thumb.
Instead of being angry,
I grinned and said **_"Yum!"_**

At recess, she painted
my face on a wall –
A terrible, horrible,
scribbly scrawl.

Instead of creating a
hullabaloo

I said:
"That's so cool –
Let me paint
your face too!"

Imogen frowned and seemed **mostly confused** –
I wasn't upset – I was acting amused.

"Hey Imogen Baddley," I said the next day,
"I brought some bananas! **Let's go out and play...**"

The look on her face...
well, I cannot explain!
Her bullying behavior had
all been in vain.

I smiled a big smile and said:
"Now that you're done

come over to
my house.
We'll play and
have fun!"

Imogen Baddley
came over to play...
I'm kind of amazed that it
turned out that way.

I think we're both lucky
I lost all control
over celery sticks
on my **cinnamon scroll.**

Sigi Cohen

Sigi Cohen was raised in South Africa and lives in Perth, Western Australia. Aside from writing for kids, Sigi works as a lawyer which he says greatly alleviates the stresses of writing children's picture books!

He is the author of the darkly funny 'My Dead Bunny', 'Filthy Fergal', 'There's Something Weird About Lena' and 'Zombie Schoolteachers'.

Sigi writes quirky stories that both children and adults enjoy reading aloud. He entertains young readers through humorous, appealing (sometimes appalling) over-the-top tales that come alive with illustrations.

Irene De La Peña

Irene De La Peña was born and raised in Madrid (Spain), where she still lives.

A lawyer by day, Irene spends her leisure time drawing for pleasure or the occassional client commission. Her dream has always been to create beautiful illustrations for children's books. Imogen Baddley is her first realisation of this dream.

A keen traveller, Irene draws to express, to let her imagination fly, to create and to escape... a little like traveling to other worlds.

Larrikin House

142-144 Frankston Dandenong Rd, Dandenong South Victoria 3175 Australia

www.larrikinhouse.com

First Published in Australia by Larrikin House 2021 (larrikinhouse.com)

Written by: Sigi Cohen
Illustrated by: Irene De La Peña
Cover Designed by: Mary Anastasiou
Design & Artwork by: Mary Anastasiou (imaginecreative.com.au)

A CIP catalogue record for this book is available from the National Library of Australia. http://catalogue.nla.gov.au

ISBN: 9781922503442 (Hardback)
ISBN: 9781922503459 (Paperback)
ISBN: 9781922503466 (Big Book)

FORESTFRIENDLY
This book is printed on paper sourced from sustainable forests

NATIONAL LIBRARY OF AUSTRALIA

A catalogue record for this book is available from the National Library of Australia